This Walker book
belongs to:

〰〰〰〰〰〰〰〰

〰〰〰〰〰〰〰〰

KT-408-393

C015348833

To my parents, with so much love.
Thank you for songs and happy memories
A

To my love Paul, thank you x
L. T.

First published 2011 by Walker Books Ltd
87 Vauxhall Walk, London SE11 5HJ

This edition published 2012

2 4 6 8 10 9 7 5 3 1

Text © 2011 Atinuke
Illustrations © 2011 Lauren Tobia

The right of Atinuke and Lauren Tobia
to be identified as author and illustrator
respectively of this work has been asserted
by them in accordance with the
Copyright, Designs and Patents Act 1988

This book has been typeset in Caslon 3

Printed in China

All rights reserved.
No part of this book may be reproduced,
transmitted or stored in an information
retrieval system in any form or by any means,
graphic, electronic or mechanical,
including photocopying, taping and recording,
without prior written permission from the publisher.

British Library Cataloguing in Publication Data:
a catalogue record for this book is available
from the British Library

ISBN 978-1-4063-3841-6

www.walker.co.uk

WALKER BOOKS
AND SUBSIDIARIES
LONDON · BOSTON · SYDNEY · AUCKLAND

ANNA HIBISCUS' SONG

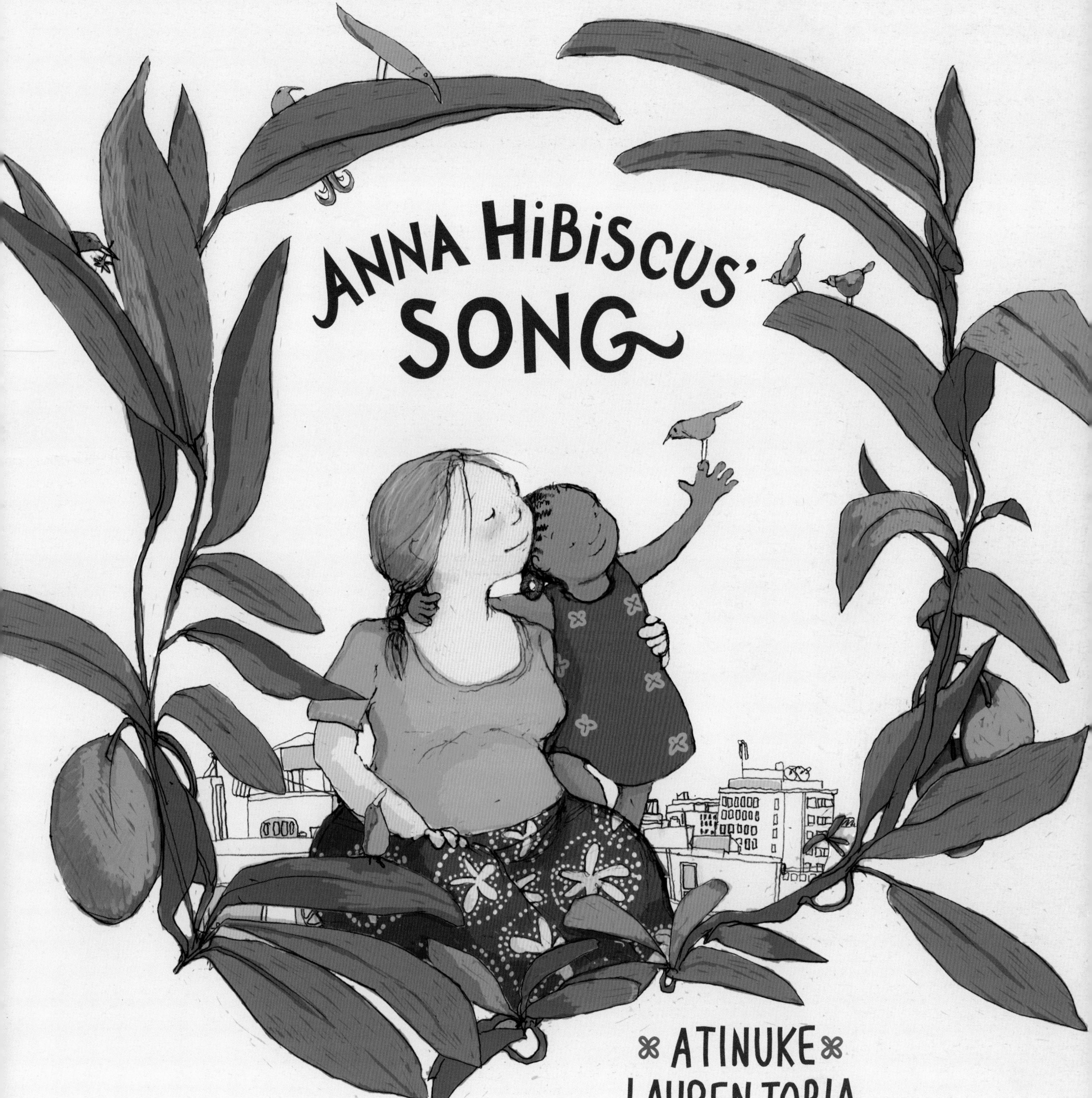

ATINUKE
LAUREN TOBIA

Anna Hibiscus lives in Africa.
Amazing Africa.

It is morning.
The sun is hot.
Anna Hibiscus is in the mango tree.
The tree is cool.

Up in the tree, Anna Hibiscus can see her whole family.

Grandmother and Grandfather are sitting on the veranda.

Aunties are pounding yam outside the kitchen.

Cousins are scattering corn for the chickens.

Papa is going to work with Uncle Tunde, and Mama is waving goodbye.

Anna Hibiscus feels so happy, she almost floats out of the tree.

Quickly, Anna Hibiscus jumps down.

"Grandmother!
Grandfather!"
Anna Hibiscus shouts.
"I'm so happy!
What can I do?"

Grandfather opens his hand wide.
"When I am happy, I count all the reasons why," he says.

Anna Hibiscus counts one, two, three, four, five fingers.
But she is far more happy than that!

"When I am happy," chuckles Grandmother,
"I squeeze Grandfather's hand."

So Anna Hibiscus does ...
and her happiness grows!

"Auntie Joli!" calls Anna Hibiscus.
"I am so happy!
What can I do?"

"You can come and help your aunties to pound yam!"
shouts Auntie Joli.

Anna Hibiscus is not sure.
"O-ya, come on!" the aunties laugh. "Our happiness
gives us the strength to work. Let us see you try!"

So Anna Hibiscus tries ...

and tries ...

and tries to pound yam.

Her aunties laugh and laugh
and laugh …

and Anna Hibiscus' happiness grows!

"Anna, come and play!" call the cousins.

So Anna Hibiscus runs to Chocolate

and Angel and Benz.

"I'm so happy!" she shouts.

"What can I do?"

Chocolate says, "When I am happy, I walk on my hands!"

"I cartwheel!" says Angel.

"I somersault!" says Benz.

So Anna Hibiscus tries
to walk on her hands ...

and cartwheel ...

and somersault …

and oh! Anna Hibiscus' happiness grows!

"Anna Hibiscus! What is going on?"
        laughs Uncle Tunde.

"Oh, Uncle Tunde!"
        says Anna Hibiscus.
"I am so happy, I don't know what to do."

"O-ya!" says Uncle Tunde, turning on the car radio.
"When I am happy, I dance!"

Uncle Tunde and Anna Hibiscus
dance and dance
around the car.

And oh!
oh!
oh!
Anna Hibiscus' happiness grows!

"Papa! Papa!
     What can I do?"
laughs Anna Hibiscus.
"I am SO happy, soon I will pop like a balloon."

"When I am happy," Papa smiles, "I go to Mama
     and tell her how much I love her."

So Anna Hibiscus runs to her mother and says
(because it is true),

"Mama, I love you so much!"

And her mother says, "I love you so much too,
Anna Hibiscus."

And oh! Anna's happiness grows SO big!

"Mama! Mama!"
cries Anna Hibiscus.
"I am so happy,
I think I am going to
EXPLODE!"

"Then sit quietly,"
smiles Anna's mother.
"I sit still and quiet
when I am happy."

Anna Hibiscus climbs back up into the mango tree.

She sits still.

She sits quiet.

"Grandfather counts
fingers and toes.

Grandmother holds
Grandfather's hand.

Aunties work, cousins play,
Uncle dances – all day long.

Papa whispers into Mama's ear.
Mama sits so quiet and still.

And me – I sing, I sing!
I sing my happiness song!"

Anna Hibiscus lives in Africa.
Amazing Africa.

Anna Hibiscus is amazing too.

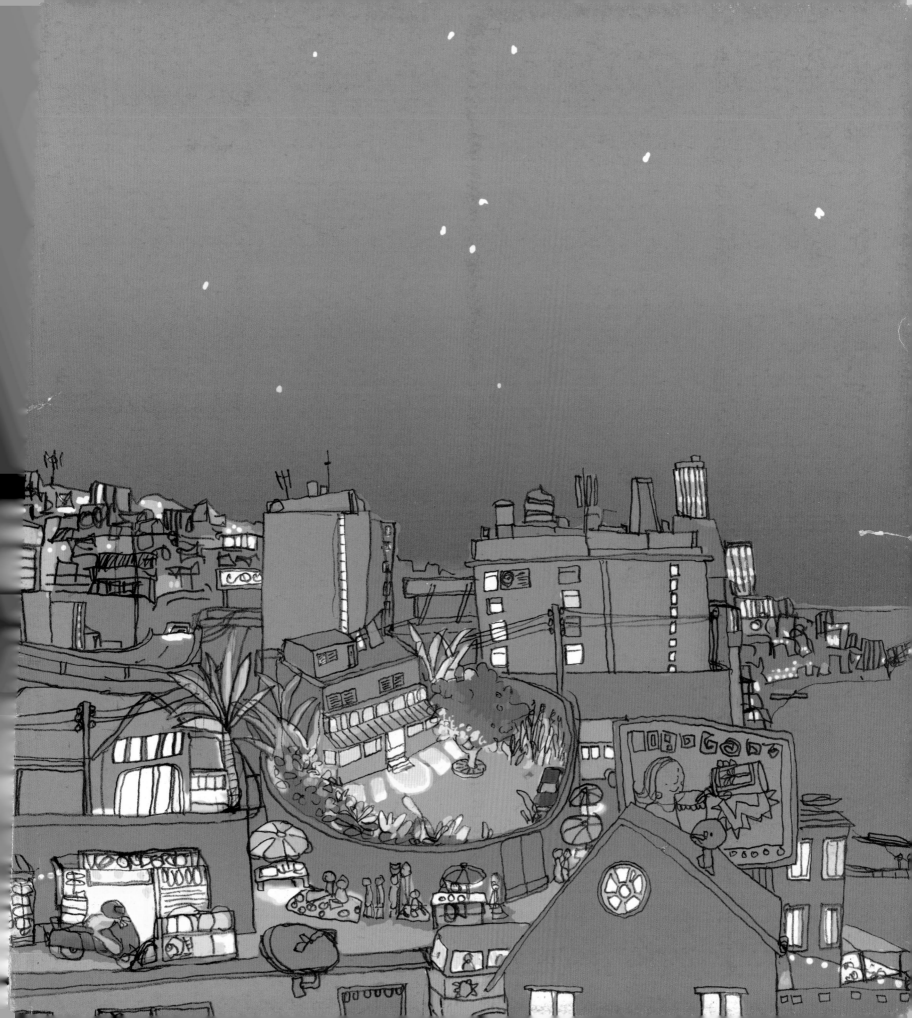

Other Anna Hibiscus books by Atinuke and Lauren Tobia:

978-1-4063-0655-2

978-1-4063-1495-3

978-1-4063-1508-0

978-1-4063-2067-1

978-1-4063-2081-7

Atinuke was born in Nigeria and spent her childhood in both Africa and the UK. Now a professional storyteller, she lives in Wales with her husband and two sons.

Lauren Tobia lives in Bristol with her husband, two daughters and two Jack Russells. When she's not busy illustrating books she loves to dig on her allotment.

Available from all good booksellers

www.walker.co.uk